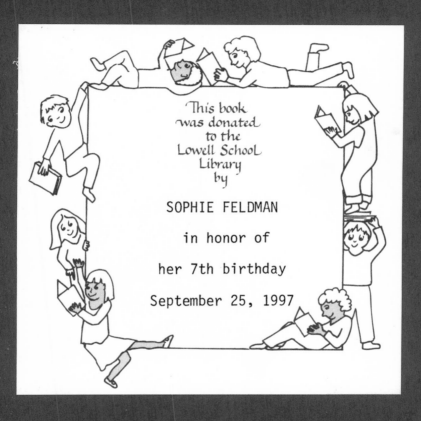

This book
was donated
to the
Lowell School
Library
by

SOPHIE FELDMAN

in honor of

her 7th birthday

September 25, 1997

SOPHIE'S LUCKY

"Here comes the horsegirl," Aunt Al said.

SOPHIE'S LUCKY

DICK KING-SMITH

illustrated by
DAVID PARKINS

CANDLEWICK PRESS
CAMBRIDGE, MASSACHUSETTS

Other books about Sophie

Sophie's Snail
Sophie's Tom
Sophie Hits Six
Sophie in the Saddle
Sophie Is Seven

Text copyright © 1995 by Fox Busters Ltd.
Illustrations copyright © 1995 by David Parkins

All rights reserved.

First U.S. edition 1996

Library of Congress Cataloging-in-Publication Data

King-Smith, Dick.
Sophie's Lucky / Dick King-Smith ; illustrated by
David Parkins.—1st U.S. ed.
Summary: A visit to great-great-aunt Al in the Scottish Highlands
leads to an exciting change in Sophie's life.
ISBN 1-56402-869-0
[1. Great-aunts—Fiction. 2. Scotland—Fiction.]
I. Parkins, David, ill. II. Title.
PZ7.K5893Sne   1996
[Fic]—dc20   95-33670

2 4 6 8 10 9 7 5 3 1

Printed in the United States

Candlewick Press
2067 Massachusetts Avenue
Cambridge, Massachusetts 02140

CONTENTS

*"What a pity, my dear," said Sophie,
"that you had to have that operation."*

In Which Sophie
Makes a Phone Call

"What a pity, my dear," said Sophie, "that you had to have that operation."

She was lying in bed, stroking the furry stomach of her black cat Tomboy, who replied with a contented purr.

A couple of years earlier Tomboy had given birth to four kittens, and that, Sophie's parents had decided, was enough.

So, despite Sophie's protests, Tomboy had been taken to the vet and spayed.

Thinking again about this as she stroked her cat, Sophie remembered how angry she had been.

"They were silly, stupid, and sickening,

they were," she said, "doing that to you. You'd have liked loads more babies, wouldn't you?"

For answer, the black cat made a noise that sounded like "Neee-o!"

Sophie looked at the four pictures on her bedroom walls—a cow, two hens, a pig, and a Shetland pony.

"Nobody's going to do operations on you, my dears," she said, "I can tell you. Blossom, you're going to have lots of calves, and April and May will have masses of chicks, and Measles will have loads of piglets, and Shorty—oh no, I forgot, you're a boy, Shorty, so you can't be a mother."

Thinking about the pony led Sophie to remember the course of riding lessons she had recently had, lessons paid for by her great, great friend, her great-great-aunt, known to all the family simply as Aunt Al.

Sophie sat up in bed with a jerk, dislodging Tomboy, who stalked out of the room, tail waving angrily.

"Aunt Al doesn't know!" she said.

She rubbed the tip of her nose, a sign of deep thought.

"I know! I'll call her up. I must tell her that I'm engaged," she said.

Sophie's best friend at school was Andrew, a stocky, fair-haired little boy to whom Sophie had recently proposed marriage.

Since her ambition had always been to become a lady farmer when grown up, and since Andrew's father had a farm, marriage —in due course—seemed to Sophie the obvious solution.

Andrew, busy watching television on the occasion of the proposal, had simply replied "Oh, all right" to everything that Sophie had said, and so was unaware of his fate.

Sophie got dressed and went downstairs.

Her twin brothers, Matthew and Mark, had already started their breakfasts. They were nine (though Matthew was ten minutes older than Mark), and life for them was a sort of race. Everything they did had to be done, it seemed, at speed, in competition with one another, and it was plain to Sophie that each was set on eating up his cornflakes before the other.

As they finished (a dead heat), the toaster popped identical twin slices, and they leaped to their feet and ran for them.

Sophie waited until her brothers had finished eating their toast (Matthew lost this race by a short crust) and gone out of the room, and then she said, "Mom, can I call Aunt Al?"

"Whatever for?"

The toaster popped identical twin slices,
and Sophie's brothers leaped to their feet.

"To tell her."

"Tell her what?"

Sophie sighed. She raised her left hand and pointed to her third finger.

"About me and Andrew, of course."

Her mother smiled.

"Wanted to wait till the boys had gone, did you?"

Sophie nodded. "They wouldn't understand," she said. "They're too inmature."

Her mother smiled.

Her father said, "Anyway, the answer is no. You are not making a long-distance phone call to the Highlands of Scotland at this time of the morning; it's too expensive, and anyway, the old lady will probably still be in bed."

Sophie's face darkened.

"She will not," she said. "She always gets up early to give Ollie his breakfast."

Ollie was a son of Tomboy, black like his mother. Sophie had given him to Aunt Al, who in return had given her great-great-niece Beano—a white rabbit with pink eyes and a wiffly nose.

"I shall just have to pay for the call myself then," said Sophie. "I'll have to use this week's pocket money for it."

Sophie's mother and father looked at their daughter, who was wearing her usual old jeans and a very old blue jersey (that was now much too small for her) with SOPHIE in white letters still dimly visible on it. They saw, under the shock of dark hair, the set expression on her face.

Then they looked at one another.

Sophie, they both knew, though small, was very determined, and it was unlikely, they both knew, that they would win this particular battle.

"This evening perhaps?" said Sophie's mother to her husband. "It's cheaper then."

"Oh, I suppose so," said Sophie's father. "And you don't have to use your precious pocket money, Sophie."

"Thanks, Mom. Thanks, Daddy," Sophie said.

Sophie did not approve of a lot of kissing or other similar displays of affection, but she got up from the table and patted her mother and rubbed the top of her head against her father's arm.

"It won't be an expensive phone call," she said. "Aunt Al's like me—she doesn't like a long conservation."

"Don't you mean conversation?" they said.

"Oh, she's all in favor of that," said Sophie. "You know, saving the rainy forests and stopping animals from becoming distinct."

*Sophie patted her mother and rubbed the top
of her head against her father's arm.*

* * *

Sophie spent quite some time that day thinking about Aunt Al, perched up there on the Highlands, surrounded by red deer and golden eagles and blue hares. She lived, Sophie knew, in a big, rambling old house called Balnacraig.

"I was born there," Aunt Al had told her once, "in 1911, and I've been there ever since. My brothers and sisters grew up and married and went away, but I stayed on to look after my mother and father. When they died, Balnacraig was left to me."

I wish I could see Aunt Al's house, Sophie thought now. I wish we could go to the Highlands one day, climb right up on the top, I mean.

"You'd like that, Puddle, wouldn't you?" she said to her dog, a small white terrier with a black patch over his right eye, and he wagged his tail in agreement. Strictly speaking, Puddle didn't belong to Sophie in the way that Tomboy and Beano did; he was the family's dog. But Sophie considered him to be hers, and he much preferred her company to anyone else's.

That evening, Sophie made sure that Matthew and Mark were busy elsewhere, and then she dialed Aunt Al's number.

As usual, she was amazed to hear that familiar voice come rushing down the steep slopes of those very high Highlands and along all those hundreds of miles of telephone wires, all in the blink of an eye.

"Hello, Aunt Al," she said. "It's me."

"Sophie!" said Aunt Al. "What a nice surprise!"

"Yes," said Sophie. "I've got another one for you too. It's about my friend Andrew."

"The farmer's son?"

17

"Yes. We're engaged to be married. I thought you'd like to know."

"That's good news," said Aunt Al. "Congratulations. By the way, how's your Farm Money going?"

For three years now Sophie had been saving up toward her ambition, and had recently persuaded her father to increase her pocket money to one pound per week.

"It was down to nine pounds and ten pence," Sophie said, "but now it's up to eleven pounds and ten pence. And I've told Andrew he's got to save fifty pence a week. By the way, how's Ollie?"

"Very well," said Aunt Al. "Would you like to see him again?"

"Oh yes," said Sophie, "but how?"

"I mentioned to your father, last time I stayed with you, that perhaps you'd all like a Scottish holiday this summer. How about coming to stay with me for a couple of weeks, what do you say to that?" said Aunt Al, and then she hastily held the receiver away from her ear as back up the hundreds of miles of wire came a loud shout of "Yikes!"

"You'll see lots of sheep," said Andrew.
"Scotch Blackfaces."

In Which Sophie
Goes Out for Dinner

On the playground at school, Sophie asked Andrew, "Have you ever been to Scotland?"

"Can't remember," Andrew said.

Sophie knew that this meant he hadn't but wasn't going to admit it. "We're going there over the summer holidays," she said.

"To stay on a farm?" asked Andrew. Last summer Sophie had, he knew, stayed on a farm in Cornwall.

"No. With my Aunt Al. On top of the Highlands."

"Sheep," said Andrew in a knowledgeable voice. "You'll see lots of sheep. Scotch Blackfaces."

21

Some boys rushed by, kicking a soccer ball, and Andrew dashed to join in. Sophie looked about for someone else who might be interested in her news, and her eyes fell upon Dawn.

Dawn, tall for her age, with golden hair done in pigtails, and dark, stocky Sophie were as different as could be. Normally Sophie would never have bothered to speak to Dawn, but now she did, remembering something that had happened recently at Cloverlea Stables. Sophie had called Dawn a wimp for being nervous of horses, and Aunt Al had told Sophie off very sharply for being unkind.

So I'll be kind now, thought Sophie, and speak to the wimp.

"Dawn!" she called.

Dawn approached, as twitchily as though Sophie were a wild bronco.

"What is it?" she said.

"Have you ever been to Scotland?" Sophie said.

"I've been to Cornwall," Dawn said nervously.

"I know that," growled Sophie (for Sophie and Dawn had met on a Cornish beach and it had not been a happy meeting), "but have you ever been to Scotland?"

"No," said Dawn.

"I'm going there, over the summer holidays."

"Oh," said Dawn.

At that point Duncan appeared. Duncan was a small, fat red-haired boy, whom Sophie had once considered as a possible worker on her farm, in due course, but he'd been fired before he'd begun. He was a very greedy little boy and he trailed about after Dawn, whose parents gave her lots of sweets.

"What about you, Duncan?" said Sophie. "Have you ever been to Scotland?"

"'Course I have," said Duncan. "I'm Scottish. Can I have a sweet, Dawn?"

"He wears a kilt," said Dawn.

"Yuck!" said Sophie. "How d'you know he does, anyway?"

"He was wearing one when he came to my party."

"What party?"

"My birthday party."

"You didn't invite me," said Sophie.

"No," said Dawn.

"Give me a sweet," said Duncan.

Dawn gave him one, and he waddled away, chewing.

Fancy him in a kilt, thought Sophie, it'd be like a miniskirt. Anyway, I wouldn't have gone to her rotten party if she'd asked me. Just wait till we're juniors and we can start doing Judo. She imagined Dawn crashing down on the mat.

"In September," she said, "I'll be doing Judo, Dawn."

Dawn looked at Sophie and knew what she was thinking. Wide-eyed, slightly buck-toothed, and with her pigtails drooping down like floppy ears, Dawn resembled a little rabbit staring helplessly at a fierce and hungry weasel.

"You'll be doing Judo, too, won't you?" said the weasel, and feebly the hypnotized rabbit answered, "Yes," but thought, *No, no!*

When school ended that day, Sophie's mother and Andrew's mother were chatting away as they waited for their children.

"I guess you know," Sophie's mother said, "that my daughter and your son are engaged to be married?"

Andrew's mother laughed.

"Are they?" she said. "He actually asked her to marry him, did he?"

"I doubt it," said Sophie's mother. "More likely she told him he was going to. Here they come now."

"You haven't asked me to dinner yet this term," Sophie was saying to Andrew.

"Well, it's only just started."

"Well, you haven't asked me."

"Why don't you ask me?" said Andrew. "Why do you always have to come over to our house?"

"Because you live on a farm, of course, silly," said Sophie, "and something's always having babies. Go on, ask your mom to ask me."

"Mom," said Andrew when he reached her, "can Sophie come over for dinner?"

"Today?"

Andrew turned to Sophie.

"Today?" he said.

Sophie nodded.

"Thanks," she said.

"Are you sure?" said Sophie's mother.

Andrew's mother nodded, smiling.

"Of course," she said, and to Sophie, "One of our best cows had a lovely pair of twins yesterday. Bull calves, unfortunately."

"Twin boys," said Sophie, shaking her head. "They're not much use. I should know."

When Andrew's father came in for his dinner before starting the evening milking, Sophie said to him, "Have you ever been to Scotland?"

"Why, yes, Sophie, years ago," he said.

"To the Highlands?"

"Yes. Wonderful country—mountains and glens and lochs. I remember once sitting by the side of Loch Ness, and what d'you think I saw?"

"The monster!" Sophie said.

Andrew's father—a keen bird-watcher—smiled.

"No," he said. "I saw a Slavonian grebe, a beautiful little diver with a black head striped with gold. I wish I had seen the monster, mind you."

"Is there one, Dad?" said Andrew.

"The local people believe there are lots. Loch Ness is a huge stretch of water, you know, twenty-four miles long and as deep as nine hundred feet in places. Plenty of room in those depths for a creature like that."

"Like what?" said Sophie.

"Probably a plesiosaurus."

"Yikes!" said Sophie. "I hope I see one."

"Are you going to Scotland then, Sophie?" said Andrew's mother.

"Yes. During the summer holidays."

"And when they're over, you and Andrew will be juniors."

"Yes, and I'll be doing Judo," said Sophie, "but they still don't give you farming lessons; I asked Matthew and Mark. You're lucky, you are, Andrew. I wish I lived on a farm."

"Perhaps one day you'll marry a farmer, Sophie," said Andrew's mother.

Sophie nodded.

"I shall," she said. "Can I have some more cake?"

The farmer and his wife looked at the two heads—one dark, one fair (almost white), each bent over a plate of cake—and then they looked at one another and smiled.

* * *

At home that evening, when her own father came up to her room to say good night,

The farmer and his wife looked at the two heads
—one dark, one fair—and smiled.

Sophie said to him, "Whereabouts in Scotland is Balnacraig, Daddy?"

"It's near Drumochter Pass, in the Grampian Mountains."

"How far from Loch Ness?"

"Oh, I suppose about twenty miles as the eagle flies. Probably a hundred by road."

"Can we go there when we're staying with Aunt Al?"

"Think we might see the monster, eh?"

"Yes, and they must want us to see them."

"Why?"

"Well," said Sophie, "Andrew's father told us. The animal is called Please-you-saw-us."

"You, my dear," said Sophie to Beano,
"are looking too fat."

In Which Sophie
Is Bowled Over

Sophie of course told both Tomboy and Puddle about the coming trip to Scotland. Tomboy, she felt sure, would be interested because of Ollie.

"I'll give him your love, my dear, never fear," said Sophie.

Puddle was to be taken with them. Sophie had been at her most determined about this.

"If he doesn't go, then I don't go," she said to her parents. "You'll have to put me in a kennel, too."

She had tried to interest Beano in the news (he had, after all, been a gift from Aunt Al), but the big white rabbit just gazed blankly at her with his pink eyes. Not for one moment would Sophie have said that Beano was stupid, but conversation with him tended to be one-sided.

Tomboy usually purred or mewed in reply to what she had to say, and Puddle wagged, or indeed barked, if she used an excited tone of voice. But Beano just wiffled his nose.

To make up for his silence, Sophie always talked to him a great deal.

One Saturday afternoon she spent a long time in the potting shed giving Beano's hutch an especially thorough cleaning and chattering busily away to him as he lolloped around on the floor.

When all was ready—his water bottle and his hay rack filled, his rabbit mixture in his feeding bowl with a nice carrot beside it, the hutch floor carpeted with fresh sawdust— Sophie stood, hands on hips, regarding her rabbit with the critical eye of a would-be lady farmer.

"You, my dear," she said, "are looking too fat. You haven't had enough exercise lately."

When Beano had first arrived, Sophie had tried exercising him on a leash. She had bought, with her Farm Money, a shiny blue collar and leash, originally for Tomboy (who didn't care for this), and in summertime she would drop the loop of the leash over a stake driven into the lawn, and Beano would graze happily around it in a circle. On the arrival of Puddle, Sophie had sold the collar and leash back to the family (for Puddle was the family's dog, not hers alone) for a profit.

"We'll borrow them back," said Sophie now to Beano. "Puddle won't mind lending them. And then I'm going to take you for a nice long walk in the garden, before it gets too dark."

In fact, taking Beano for a walk meant being taken for a walk by Beano, who was only interested in going his own way. The big rabbit was strong, and he towed Sophie around the garden, to the amusement of Matthew and Mark, who were still, in the fading light, playing one-a-side soccer on the lawn—two bamboo poles were stuck in the grass at either end, as goals.

Suddenly, Beano took it into his head to try to run across the playing field, while Sophie hauled on his leash to no avail.

At the same time one of the boys took a shot at the goal, and the ball struck Sophie full on the side of her head. Dazed, she fell to her knees, letting go of the leash.

"Gosh, sorry, Sophie!" the kicker cried, and "He didn't mean to!" cried his opponent, and they both squatted anxiously beside their sister.

The ball struck Sophie full on the side of her head.

"Don't cry," they said.

"I'm not," said Sophie.

Sophie did not approve of crying.

"Are you all right?" they said.

Sophie shook her head.

"I feel a bit dizzy," she said.

"You better come inside," said Mark.

"And sit down for a bit," said Matthew, and they each took one of Sophie's arms and raised her up and marched her off the field.

"Mom!" they shouted. "Sophie's injured!"

Then they explained what had happened, and Mark said that it was he who had kicked the ball, and Matthew said that Mark hadn't meant to hurt Sophie, and Sophie said she had a bit of a headache, and their mother said that Sophie had better lie down on the sofa for a bit. Which she did.

But after a while she suddenly remembered—Beano! She'd dropped the leash when the ball hit her. Beano was still out in the dark garden.

"Quick!" she shouted, leaping to her feet. "We must find him!"

"Find who?" they all said.

"My rabbit. He's loose in the garden!" cried Sophie, and she rushed out.

"Go with her, boys," their mother said, "while I make sure the gate to the road is shut, and then I'll come and help you look."

By now it was quite dark, and though they all searched for ages with a flashlight—over the lawn, in the flower beds, in the vegetable patch, and through the shrubbery—there was no sign of Beano.

"Perhaps he's hopped back into the potting shed," said Sophie's mother. But he hadn't. There in the flashlight beam was his hutch, beautifully clean but quite empty. He had simply disappeared.

"The gate was shut, wasn't it, Mom?" said Sophie.

"Yes."

"He must be somewhere in the garden," Sophie said.

"Of course he is. We'll find him, don't worry. Let's all go and have some dinner now—it's getting rather cold out here—and then we'll have another search, and I expect he'll have come out from wherever he's hiding."

Sophie would not eat any dinner.

"I couldn't," she said. "Not when Beano hasn't had his."

Afterward all five of them—for the children's father had returned from the golf club—put on coats (it was beginning to get cold) and mounted another search, but in vain.

At last they gave up—at least, four of

them did. Sophie plodded doggedly on, prepared to go on all night if need be. But, for once, her parents proved more determined than she was and insisted that she go to bed.

"There's nothing more we can do tonight," they said. "You snuggle down and go to sleep now, there's a good girl."

"I couldn't," Sophie said. "Not while Beano's out in the cold."

For a long time she didn't, but then at last, tired out, she fell deeply asleep.

Sophie woke early the following morning with the feeling that something was terribly wrong, and ᵗhen she remembered and jump͢ d and ran to the window.

It w ᵗng light, and the lawn, she cou ⸝hite with frost. But on it there v ⸝hite lolloping shape. Nothing he garden below, except—what was that? Something was moving, along the top of the garden wall, some animal, the size of a small dog or a large cat. It walked along the wall and then stopped and sat there, looking down toward the potting shed. It was reddish in color— Sophie could see now as the light grew stronger—and it had a sharp pointed face and a bushy tail. It was a fox!

Before Sophie could think what to do, another animal appeared: a white one. Out from beneath the potting shed, under which he had burrowed last evening to spend a comfortable night, emerged Beano. He hopped out onto the lawn, the blue collar around his neck, the blue leash trailing behind him, and sniffed curiously at the frosted grass. Each hop took him nearer to the watching fox.

"Look out, Beano, look out!" yelled

It was a fox!

Sophie at the top of her voice, but the double panes of her window deadened the sound. The fox slipped down from the wall top, eyes fixed upon the approaching rabbit.

At that instant a third animal appeared upon the scene: a black animal, an angry animal, furious at the sight and the rank smell of this red, bushy-tailed intruder in her garden.

Tomboy's ears were flat upon her head, her back arched, her coat standing on end, and suddenly she launched herself, spitting and yowling, straight at the fox, which turned tail and leaped back over the wall and was gone.

Matthew and Mark had slept through Sophie's loud shout, but it had woken her mother and father from their Sunday morning sleep-in, and now they looked from their window to see Sophie, in bathrobe and slippers, being towed by Beano back to the potting shed and his nice clean hutch and his supper-become-breakfast.

Behind them, her tail raised high in triumph, her coat very black against the frosty grass, stalked Sophie's victorious Tomboy.

"I'm sorry, my dear," Sophie told Tomboy.
"This is all they'd let me have."

IN WHICH SOPHIE
DREAMS A DREAM

At breakfast Sophie said to the others, "Yikes! You should have seen it! Tomboy was as fierce as a tiger! He was intimated, that old fox was."

"You mean he was intimidated," her father said.

"I mean he was absolutely putrified."

"Petrified," said her mother.

"Call it what you like," said Sophie. "He was scared stiff."

The twins paused in the middle of their cornflake race for Matthew to say, "Good old Tomboy," and Mark to say, "Lucky old Beano," before they went on shoveling the stuff in.

"Imagine your cat saving your rabbit's life," said Sophie's mother, and her father said, "You ought to reward her. Give her something nice to eat. What does she like best?"

"Fish," Sophie said. "She likes fish."

"What sort?"

Matthew swallowed hastily, winning the race by a short flake, and said, "I know!"

Mark swallowed, too, and said, "I know what you're going to say!" and together they chanted, "Sardines in tomato sauce!"

"Yuck!" said Sophie. That was her least favorite food. "Don't be so silly, stupid, and sickening," she went on, automatically but not in anger. "Sardines in tomato sauce are indelible."

"Indelible?" said her mother.

"Inedible," said her father.

"Mommy," said Sophie. "Got any fish fingers?"

"There's a packet in the freezer. You can have one for Tomboy if you like."

"Only one?" said Sophie. "That's mean."

"All right, two then."

Later, in the potting shed, Sophie said, "I'm sorry, my dear, this is all they'd let me have."

She stroked Tomboy, and went on. "I put them under the cushion in Dad's chair when he wasn't looking, and he'd been sitting on them all the time he was reading the Sunday papers, so they should have unfrozen nicely."

She sat watching her cat eating, and then she let Beano out of his hutch, and put on the collar and leash once more. The boys, she knew, had gone to play with friends, so there would be no danger from flying soccer balls.

"And don't worry about that old fox," she

said to her rabbit. "He won't come back in a hurry."

The sun was shining, the frost was gone, and there was a feeling in the air that spring was only just around the corner.

Beano must have felt this, for he jumped about in a very bouncy way, while Puddle barked approvingly, and Tomboy lay in a patch of sunshine and licked the last of the fish fingers from her lips.

After a while Sophie tied Beano's leash to the leg of a garden seat and sat down, while Puddle jumped up beside her.

She looked in turn at her three animals and thought how lucky she was to have them.

"But I must tell you, my dear," she said to Puddle, rubbing the base of his ears—something he especially liked—"that there is another animal I would very much like to have. It has four legs with hooves on the end of them, and a mane and a tail, and you can ride on it, and it's got four letters, beginning with P and ending in Y. Can you guess?"

Puddle gave a yap.

"I thought you could," Sophie said. "I just wish I could have one of my own, but I don't suppose I'll ever be that lucky."

Just then Tomboy stood up and stretched herself, and then padded across the lawn— from right to left—in front of the garden seat. "Yikes!" said Sophie softly to Puddle. "A black cat coming from the right-hand side is always lucky. Aunt Al told me that ages ago."

When she had put Beano back in his hutch, Sophie plodded off to find her mother.

"Mommy," she said. "I'm a good rider, aren't I? Meg Morris said so."

Meg Morris was the owner of Cloverlea Stables, and also of Dolly, Tomboy's only daughter.

"Yes, Sophie," her mother said. "You ride very well."

"Well then, d'you think I'll ever have a pony of my own?"

"Before you get to be a lady farmer, d'you mean?"

"Yes. While I'm still young."

"Do you want an honest answer?"

"Yes."

"No."

"Oh."

"To begin with, we've nowhere to put a pony. Second, they're very expensive to buy in any case, and to keep. I'm sorry, Sophie love, but I'm afraid you'll just have to forget the idea."

Sophie nodded.

"I just thought I'd ask," she said.

"Tell you what," her mother said. "It'll be the Easter holidays soon, and then I'll pay for you to have a ride on one of Meg Morris's ponies. Would you like that?"

"Yes, please," said Sophie.

She patted her mother, which meant "Thank you very much," and then she said, "Do they have riding stables anywhere near where Aunt Al lives?"

"I don't know."

"Perhaps she's got a pony. She did have one once, called Frisk, but that was in 1920, so I expect he'll have died."

Sophie's mother smiled. "They certainly used to keep horses at Balnacraig," she said. "I remember seeing the stable, with a little white clock tower on top. Daddy and I had our honeymoon in Scotland, and we went to visit Aunt Al while we were there.

"I've seen pictures of Highland cattle," said Sophie.

We walked around the farm."

"What farm?" said Sophie.

"Hers."

"She never told me she was a lady farmer," said Sophie.

"She isn't," her mother said. "The land belongs to her but it is rented to a neighboring farmer. In the old days, Aunt Al's father used to breed Highland cattle, I believe."

"I've seen pictures of them! They've got long tously hair," said shaggy Sophie, "and long horns, and they're a lovely golden color."

"That's right."

"How big is the farm?" said Sophie.

"I don't really know. Smallish for Scotland, I think."

"How long is it before we go to Scotland?"

"Oh, goodness, it's more than three months away. You'll just have to be patient. Remember the old rhyme:

Patience is a Virtue.
Virtue is a Grace.
Grace is a little girl
Who wouldn't wash her face."

Grace sounded much nicer than Dawn, Sophie thought. Dawn was probably always washing her face.

She rubbed the tip of her nose.

"Mom," she said, "when I'm old enough, d'you think Aunt Al would rent the farm to me?"

"Sophie, my love," her mother said, "you're not eight yet, and Aunt Al's going to be eighty-three in the autumn. So if you're talking about when you're twenty, let's say, then Aunt Al would be . . . let me see . . . ninety-five!"

"That's okay," said Sophie. "She told me she's going to live to be a hundred."

Grinning all over her face, Sophie drew from her pocket a blue ribbon.

In Which Sophie
Wins a Prize

When the Easter holidays began, Sophie was not slow to remind her mother of her promise. Before breakfast on the very first morning she said, "Will you be phoning the stables today?"

"The stables?"

"Yes. Cloverlea Stables. *You* know."

"Oh yes, of course," said her mother, and after breakfast she did.

Sophie did not listen to her mother talking on the telephone. She sat in another room with her fingers crossed, and only when she heard the *ting!* as her mother hung up did she go to her and say, "Well?"

"Well," said Sophie's mother, "Meg's a bit busy at the moment, organizing an event called 'Own-a-Pony-for-a-Day.'"

"What's that?" said Sophie.

"It's a whole day event that she runs— first a grooming competition, then a treasure hunt on foot, then a quiz, then a riding lesson, and then in the afternoon, after a picnic lunch, there's a riding contest. It would be a lucky child who could do all that, wouldn't it?"

"It would," said Sophie.

"Well, you're a lucky child."

"Yikes!" shouted Sophie. "Wicked! Mommy, you're ace!"

When the great day came, Sophie had a marvelous time. There were nine other girls and three boys, and Meg Morris gave them each a number to wear. Sophie was Number Thirteen.

She certainly didn't have any luck in the morning. Some of the other children were quite a bit older, and could reach higher up on their ponies when grooming them, and run faster in the treasure hunt on foot, and answer harder questions in the quiz.

But in the afternoon it was different.

Back home afterward, everyone wanted to know how well Sophie had done.

"Did you win a prize?" asked Mark.

Sophie nodded.

"What for?" asked Matthew.

"The riding contest," said Sophie.

"What did you win?" asked Sophie's father.

"Oh, just a ribbon," said Sophie off-handedly.

"Oh, what color was it?" her father asked.

"What does it matter what color it was?" asked the twins.

"There are different ones, for first, second, third, or fourth prize." he said. "I can't remember exactly which is which. Tell us, Sophie."

"Green is for fourth place," Sophie said. "Yellow is for third. Red is for second. And blue is for first."

"Well, go on, tell us," everyone said. "What color was yours?"

Sophie, grinning all over her face, drew from her pocket a blue ribbon.

Sophie's triumph at "Own-a-Pony-for-a-Day" was matched, during the spring term, by the twins' customary successes on the school's field day. Matthew and Mark were forever racing one another, and as usual they beat the other boys in most of the races.

Sophie was not much good at running,

though once, when she was five, she had won the egg-and-spoon race. This year she didn't win anything (though she tried hard enough), but she didn't mind too much. To have won that blue ribbon at the riding contest had been enough. She had stuck it to her bedroom wall with Blu-Tack, underneath the picture of Shorty.

"I'm sorry, my dears," she said to Blossom, April, May, and Measles, "but it has to go with a horse, even though it is rather a short horse."

Anyway, Sophie's mind hadn't really been on field day. All she could think about was that in a week's time the spring term would be over at long last, and then they would all be setting off to stay with Aunt Al.

As the day of departure drew near, the children's father got out his road atlas to show them where they were going.

"It's a heck of a long way," he said. "It'll take us a couple of days."

"How far is it?" they said.

"About six hundred miles."

"If you went at sixty miles an hour . . ." said Matthew.

". . . we'd be there in ten hours," said Mark.

Sophie watched her father's finger tracing the route on the map, from quite near the bottom of England to quite near the top of Scotland.

"Don't be silly," she said to her brothers. "You can't go up to Scotland at sixty miles an hour. Can't you see—it's uphill, all the way to the top of the Highlands."

"It's not," they said. "It's just going from south to north."

"Exactly," said Sophie. "Going up. After all, you wouldn't say 'I'm going *down* to the North Pole,' would you?"

No amount of explanation would change Sophie's mind about this, and when they did set off on the long drive, she remarked at regular intervals that it would be better on the return journey, they'd be going downhill all the way.

In fact, when at last the family arrived at Balnacraig, Sophie was fast asleep in her seat belt.

"Wake up, Sophie!" they all said. "We're here."

Sophie opened her eyes to see that they had drawn up on a sweep of gravel before a tall gray house. It had a great many long, narrow windows and, above a flight of stone steps, a massive oak front door, which now opened to show a familiar small figure.

Aunt Al came down the steps on her thin bird's legs to greet them all—the grown-ups with a kiss, the boys with a hug. She

*A massive oak front door opened
to show a familiar small figure.*

came to Sophie last, looking, with her sharp blue eyes and her thin beaky nose, more birdlike than ever, and, knowing Sophie, attempted neither kiss nor hug, but held out her hand, bony and curled like a bird's claw. Sophie took it.

"How de do, Sophie?" said Aunt Al, and, "I'm very well," said Sophie, and they grinned at one another.

The children spent the rest of that first day exploring the many tall dark rooms of the old house, right up to the attics that ran the length of it beneath its steep slate roof, decorated with many strange turrets and battlements.

Then there was the stable, with its clock tower above, and inside, a double row of stalls divided by wooden partitions topped with iron railings.

On some of the doors, names were still

dimly visible—MAJOR, STARLIGHT, DUCHESS
—and on one, Sophie saw with delight, was
written FRISK. There were no horses within
now, no stamp of hooves upon the cobbled
floor; but the smell was still there, Sophie
thought, a faint smell of horse and hay and
harness.

Last thing that night, Aunt Al came up to
say good night, in the little attic bedroom
which was to be Sophie's for the holiday,
and Sophie said to her, "You never told me
you were a lady farmer."

"Well, I'm not, strictly speaking," said
Aunt Al. "The land that I own is rented out
to a neighboring farmer, Mr. Grant."

"How much land?" said Sophie.

"Not a lot. Just over a hundred and
fifty acres."

"Yikes!" said Sophie softly. "That's a lot.
Can we go and see it tomorrow?"

"If you like."

"Just you and me?"

"I dare say it will be just you and me," said Aunt Al. "I know your mother is looking forward to taking things easy and putting her feet up a bit, and your father will want to go down to the loch."

"Loch Ness?"

"No, no, just a wee lochan, but there are fish to be had, and I know he's keen to teach Matthew and Mark how to handle a rod. So you and I will walk down to the farm and see Mr. Grant."

And after breakfast next morning they did.

Mr. Grant was big and Mrs. Grant was small, and both of them had the sort of smiling faces that made Sophie like them right away.

"This is my great-great-niece," Aunt Al said.

*The farmer lead out a stocky brown pony that looked
as if it had just come through a hedge backward.*

"She has a wee bit of a look of you about her, Miss Alice," said Mrs. Grant. "Maybe not the features so much, but the expression. A determined person, I'd say."

"You'd be right," said Aunt Al. And to Mr. Grant she said, "Is Lucky ready?"

"He is," said Mr. Grant, and he went off across the yard.

"Who's Lucky?" said Sophie.

"He belongs to Mr. and Mrs. Grant's daughter," said Aunt Al, "but she's grown out of him, and they've very kindly agreed to lend him to you while you're here. Look."

And Sophie looked and saw the farmer leading out a stocky brown pony that looked as if it had just come through a hedge backward. As a delighted Sophie stood at his head, patting him and telling him what a fine fellow he was, there was quite a likeness between them.

"His coat's a mess, Miss Alice," said Mr. Grant. "He wants grooming badly. But you told me that . . ."

"I told you," said Aunt Al, "that if Sophie is going to ride him, then she's going to groom him. Okay, Sophie?"

"Okay!" said Sophie. And to the farmer she said, "Please, I shall want some warm water and a body brush and a curry comb and a dandy brush." She grabbed Lucky's halter and said, "Walk on!" in so determined a voice that the pony immediately obeyed.

"I was right," said Mrs. Grant.

Later that morning, Sophie, wearing a hard hat that had belonged to the Grants' daughter, rode Lucky up the long drive to Balnacraig. Mr. Grant had already driven Aunt Al home because she was feeling a bit tired, and she was sitting in a chair on the lawn with Sophie's mother.

"Here comes the horsegirl," she said.

"What a nice sturdy little pony," said Sophie's mother. "Apart from the difference in color, he reminds me of Bumblebee that Sophie rode in Cornwall."

"Lucky suits her well," said Aunt Al. "Perhaps the Grants would sell him to you."

"Oh, Aunt Al!" laughed Sophie's mother. "Wherever would we keep him? Even if we could afford him."

"Ah well," said Aunt Al. "You never know."

*To look at, Mrs. McCosh was
the opposite of Aunt Al.*

In Which Sophie
Hears Sad News

Sophie never forgot those ten August days
spent at Balnacraig. She had Lucky to ride,
with Puddle running beside them, and she
had big black Ollie to pet, and the weather
was fine, the scenery was beautiful, and on
top of all that they were very well fed by
Aunt Al's housekeeper, Mrs. McCosh.

Mrs. McCosh had been with Aunt Al's
family all her working life.

"She started as a young girl, helping in
the kitchen, while my parents were still
alive," Aunt Al told Sophie, "and then later
she turned out to be a splendid cook. Now
she looks after the house, and me, too, for

I'm not as young as I was. I don't know what I'd do without Eilie McCosh."

"What about Mr. McCosh?" Sophie asked. "Is he dead?"

"Well," said Aunt Al, "between you and me and the gatepost, he was never actually alive. You see, Eilie never married, but she likes to be known as 'Mrs.' McCosh. It sounds right for a housekeeper, she says."

"She makes yummy cakes," Sophie said. "And she lets me lick the bowls."

Sophie and the housekeeper had hit it off immediately. To look at, Mrs. McCosh was the opposite of Aunt Al. She was large, with a round brown face and strong arms and sturdy legs. If Aunt Al looked like a little bird, Mrs. McCosh was more of a big teddy bear.

"I'll tell you something, Sophie," she said one day. "Miss Alice is very fond of your daddy—he's the only member of her family that bothers about her—and of your mother, of course, and your brothers, too. But you're her favorite, anyone with half an eye can see that."

Sophie felt very pleased at this. "She's my favorite great-great-aunt," she said.

"How many great-great-aunts do you have?"

"Just her. She's going to live to be a hundred, did you know?"

"Is that what Miss Alice told you?"

"Yes."

On the last afternoon of their stay, Sophie asked Aunt Al if she would like to go for a walk and Aunt Al said she would, but not too far.

"You feeling tired then?" asked Sophie.

"A bit."

"It must be tiring having us all staying."

Aunt Al smiled.

"No, it's not that," she said.

"Can we go as far as the farm?" Sophie asked. "I want to say good-bye to Lucky."

"Of course," said Aunt Al.

At the farm Mr. and Mrs. Grant came out to say their good-byes.

"So you're away home tomorrow?" Mrs. Grant said to Sophie.

"Yes," said Sophie. "I don't want to go. I shall miss Lucky like anything."

"He'll miss you," said Mr. Grant. "He's taken quite a fancy to you."

Sophie stroked Lucky's velvety muzzle. "I wish you were mine," she said.

"One of these fine days," said Aunt Al, "you might have a pony of your own."

"Miss Alice is right," said Mr. Grant. "You might be lucky, too."

"Imagine living on that nice farm," said Sophie as they walked home. They reached

*Sophie stroked Lucky's velvety muzzle.
"I wish you were mine," she said.*

a rough seat that stood by the side of the drive, and Aunt Al sat down for a moment to rest.

"D'you think you would like living there one day, Sophie?" she said.

"I would!" exclaimed Sophie. "But I'd need an awful lot of Farm Money to buy it, wouldn't I?"

"You might," said Aunt Al, "and then again, you might not."

That evening, Mrs. McCosh produced a splendid supper, which included two fine trout—one caught by Matthew, one by Mark. These were the young anglers' very first catches, and no one was surprised that the fish were of an identical size and weight.

"It's been a wonderful holiday, Aunt Al," Sophie's father said.

"Marvelous," said her mother. "Hasn't it, children?"

"Great," said the twins with their mouths full.

Sophie didn't say anything.

"Well, Sophie?" said her mother.

"I would like to live here," said Sophie simply.

"I would like it very much if you did," said Aunt Al, "and so, I think, would Mrs. McCosh. She tells me you have the makings of a cook."

"But I fear," said Sophie's father, "that tomorrow we must all head home. Perhaps, Aunt Al, you could come and visit us again before long?"

"I shall look forward to that," said Aunt Al.

"It's downhill all the way," said Sophie.

Early next morning they were on their way.

Sophie didn't like good-byes, and when

her turn came, she was going to stick out her hand as usual. But then suddenly—she didn't know why—she rushed and flung her arms around Aunt Al's skinny middle.

Then they were off, down the long drive of Balnacraig, while behind them two figures—one small and birdlike, one large and bearlike—stood waving farewell, while Ollie rubbed himself against their different-sized legs.

Two days later Tomboy was doing the same thing to Sophie. She seemed pleased to see her back, and Beano, Sophie thought, wiffled his nose more than usual. The next-door neighbor, Sophie decided, had looked after them well.

Matthew and Mark, fishing forgotten for now, thought only of soccer and their chances of playing for the school in the coming term. Sophie had no such ambitions

*Tomboy seemed pleased to see Sophie back,
and Beano wiffled his nose more than usual.*

about volleyball. Small and determined though she was, she knew that in this game it was an advantage to be a beanpole like Dawn. But she was looking forward to the start of the term, for she would now be a junior and could, at last, do Judo. I don't suppose Dawn will do it though, she thought. Pity.

Some weeks after the children had gone back to school, the family was sitting in the kitchen having breakfast, when the phone rang. Sophie's father got up and went out of the room to answer it. He was away some time, and when he returned, the three children had gone to get ready for school.

Sophie's mother took one look at her husband's face and said, "What is it?"

"That was Mrs. McCosh," said Sophie's father heavily, "calling from Balnacraig."

"Aunt Al—she's ill? What did Mrs. McCosh say?"

"She said, 'I'm sorry to have to tell you that Miss Alice died last night.'"

"Oh, no!"

"It was all very peaceful apparently. She had told Mrs. McCosh she was feeling a bit tired and would go to bed early, and she just died in her sleep. Not a bad way to go."

"We must tell the children."

"Not now. Let's get them off to school, and we'll tell them this evening."

When the time came, Sophie's father didn't beat around the bush. Sophie and the two boys were watching television, and as their program finished, he switched the set off and said, "Listen, all of you. I'm afraid there's some sad news. Aunt Al has died."

They stared at him for a moment, and

then Matthew said, "When did she die?"

"Last night."

"What did she die of?" asked Mark.

"Old age, I suppose we must say. She was nearly eighty-three, you know."

"But she told me she was going to live to be a hundred," Sophie said.

"I'm afraid she was wrong, Sophie love," said her mother. "She died very peacefully, Mrs. McCosh said, just slipped away in her sleep. You must try not to be too sad, she wouldn't have wanted you to be."

For a little while the children said nothing—Matthew and Mark because they couldn't think what to say, and Sophie because she had a big lump in her throat.

After a minute she said gruffly, "What about Ollie?"

"Oh, I'm sure Mrs. McCosh will look after Ollie," her father said.

Sophie nodded. Then she got up and went out of the room.

Looking through the window, they saw her plodding down the path to the potting shed.

Inside it, Sophie stood looking at the big white rabbit that had been a gift from her great-great-aunt.

She remembered the day when she and Aunt Al had walked down to the potting shed together, and Aunt Al had said, "Shut your eyes, Sophie," and Sophie had said, "Why?" And then, once they were inside, Aunt Al had said, "Surprise! You can look now."

And when she had opened her eyes, there was Beano!

Now, as she looked at him, her eyes filled.

Then she sniffed loudly, twice.

Then, even though she had never approved of crying, Sophie burst out into a really good howl.

The little church was full.

In Which Sophie
Says Good-Bye

The following week Sophie's father drove up to Scotland once again, this time for his great-aunt's funeral. To take the children out of school for another twelve-hundred-mile roundtrip was not, they decided, a good idea, so Sophie's mother stayed behind to look after them all.

"What's more," he said, "I have to come back via London. Aunt Al's lawyers want to see me about her will."

When at last he reached home again—quite late one evening, while the children were all fast asleep—Sophie's mother said, "You must be worn out. How did it all go?"

"The funeral, you mean? I was surprised. The little church was full. Lots of local people, and Mrs. McCosh of course, and Mr. and Mrs. Grant the farmers. Aunt Al was very well liked, it's plain."

"No one from the family?"

"Only me."

"And you went to see the lawyers?"

"Yes, I did. You had better sit down."

"Why?"

"Apart from a bequest to Mrs. McCosh, Aunt Al has left her entire estate to us."

Sophie's mother did sit down—with a bump.

"Balnacraig, you mean?"

"Everything," said Sophie's father. "The house and grounds, the contents of the house, the farm, and all her money—which is a great deal. My great-aunt was, it seems, a very rich old lady. She changed her will

Sophie's mother did sit down—with a bump.

quite recently, the lawyer told me, and she has made a special provision for our children, too. There's a large sum of money in trust for Matthew and an exactly similar amount, you'll not be surprised to hear, for Mark. They'll have the use of it at eighteen."

"And Sophie?"

"No money for Sophie. Something that will please her much more."

"What?"

"The farm at Balnacraig. Mr. Grant is to continue as tenant until Sophie reaches the age of eighteen, and then, if she still wishes, she will realize her ambition."

"To be a lady farmer!"

"If she's changed her mind by then, well, it will be hers to sell."

"She won't change her mind!"

"There is something that I haven't told you, though," said Sophie's father to his wife.

"All this—the property, the money, the children's share in it, everything—depends upon one condition. Which is that we do not sell Aunt Al's house, but move to Scotland and live in Balnacraig ourselves."

"Oh!" said Sophie's mother. "That would be wonderful. But . . ."

"But what?"

"Our friends here—the children's school —your job."

"We shall make other friends, and Scottish schools are very good, and it's quite possible my firm might have a job for me up there. If not, I'll find another. Anyway, we shan't starve!"

Next day they said to the children, "We're thinking of moving."

"Where to?" said Mark.

"Scotland."

"Where in Scotland?" said Matthew.

"To the Highlands."

"Where in the Highlands?" said Sophie.

"Balnacraig. Aunt Al has left the house to us in her will. It's ours now!"

Matthew and Mark positively gabbled with excitement. Could they have their own fishing rods, could they learn to ski, could they go mountaineering, could they go to Hampden Park to see the soccer internationals, how soon could they move?

Somehow or other—they never knew how they managed it—Sophie's father and mother did all the things that had to be done to be ready for the move at the end of the autumn term.

By now they had told the boys that Aunt Al had left them each a sum of money for when they were grown up.

"Wow!" they said.

"How much?" said Matthew.

"A lot."

"A hundred pounds?" said Mark.

"A bit more than that."

"What about Sophie?" they said.

"Oh, she's been left something, too."

Later, her parents asked Sophie whether she liked the idea of going to live at Balnacraig.

"I told you before," said Sophie. "I would like to live there. Very much. But I'm not coming unless Tomboy and Beano and Puddle come, too."

"Of course they will."

"Will Mrs. McCosh still be there?"

"We'll have to see. She may want to retire."

"She can't take Ollie," said Sophie. "He is Tomboy's son, remember, and I bred him and I gave him to Aunt Al, and I'm sure she would want me to have him now. So will Ollie be mine?"

"If you like."

"And shall I be able to ride Lucky?"

"I'm sure Mr. Grant will let you."

"Okay," said Sophie. "I'll come."

At last everything was settled. They had found a buyer for their house, they made all the arrangements for the removal of everything they were taking with them, and they settled upon a new school for the children, not far from Balnacraig.

"It'll feel funny to be leaving your friends," Sophie's mother said to her, "but you'll soon make other ones. Still, I guess you'll miss some of the children, won't you?"

"Not Dawn," said Sophie. "Nor Duncan," she added.

"But what about Andrew? I thought you were engaged to him."

"He could always come to stay," said Sophie.

"It's rather a long way to come. He might not want to."

"He will. I'll tell him, when I go to dinner with him tomorrow."

"On the last day of term? Has Andrew's mother invited you?"

"No, but she will. I'll tell him to tell her to."

And she did.

And he did.

At the farm, Andrew's father and mother asked Sophie all about Balnacraig, but after dinner Andrew seemed more interested in watching sports on TV. He did not seem too bothered that his fiancée was about to go and live six hundred miles away, and only made his usual reply to her remarks.

"Next year," Sophie said to him, "you can come and stay in Scotland."

"Oh, all right."

"And mind you keep on saving up your pocket money."

"What for?"

"So that we'll have a nice home when we get married, of course."

"Oh, all right."

When Sophie's mother arrived to collect her, Andrew was still glued to the television set.

"Andrew!" his mother said. "Sophie's going. Aren't you coming to say good-bye?"

At the front door, the engaged couple stood facing one another.

"You'll miss Sophie, won't you, Andrew?" his mother said.

Andrew nodded.

"Good-bye," he said.

It was plain he was anxious to get back to his program.

"Now don't forget what I told you," said Sophie.

*At the front door, the engaged couple
stood facing one another.*

"What about?"

"About the money. Saving. *You* know."

"Oh, all right."

"The trouble with Andrew," said Sophie to her mother as they made their way home, "is that he doesn't consecrate."

"Concentrate, you mean."

"I mean, he doesn't listen to what I say."

"Perhaps you'd better not marry him then."

"I shan't," said Sophie, "unless he gets his father's farm when he's grown up."

"But just suppose," said her mother, "that when *you're* grown up, you should have a farm of your own?"

"Oh, well then," said Sophie, "I wouldn't need to marry Andrew. Because I'd be a lady farmer, wouldn't I?"

"You will," her mother said. "The boys probably never told you, but Aunt Al left them a lot of money."

But not me, thought Sophie. Funny, she knew I needed more Farm Money.

"She left you something, too, for when you're grown up."

"What?" said Sophie.

"The farm at Balnacraig."

Everyone was dog tired (including Puddle).

In Which
Sophie's Lucky

On Christmas Day—Sophie's eighth birthday—the three children were given only
small presents. They didn't mind, because
they'd been told that when, in a week's time,
they made the move to Scotland, there
would be a very special present waiting for
each of them at the other end.

"And don't think you'll get such presents
every year," their father told them. "These
are to celebrate our coming to Balnacraig to
live."

When at last they all arrived at their new
home, it was very late and everyone was

dog tired (including Puddle). Mrs. McCosh, who had said she would stay on as long as they wanted her, had supper ready, and afterward the children went to bed. No amount of pleading would persuade their parents to show them those three special presents that night.

"First thing after breakfast tomorrow," their father said. "I promise."

Sophie lay in bed in her new room, the little attic bedroom where she had slept when Aunt Al was still alive, and looked at her pictures, newly hung up on the walls, of Blossom, April May, Measles, and Shorty.

Tired as she was, her last thoughts before sleep were of her animals. Puddle was in his bed in the kitchen. Beano was in his hutch in a loose box, a warmer and drier place than the old potting shed. As for Tomboy, Sophie knew that Ollie was busy showing his mother around the place. All was well.

First thing after breakfast the next morning, Sophie's father said, "Right. Time now for your rather late Christmas presents, and Sophie, yours will be Christmas and birthday combined."

"Where are they?" the children asked.

"In the stable," their mother said, "but no rushing ahead, mind. We'll all go down together."

So they did, and there, just inside the main door of the stable, were two brand-new mountain bikes—one red, one blue.

"The red one's for you, Matthew," said his father.

"And," said his mother, "the blue one's for you, Mark."

"Oh, thanks! Thanks a million!" they shouted, and each grabbed hold of his bike and dashed off.

Each twin grabbed hold of his bike and dashed off.

Sophie looked around, but she couldn't see any sign of a present for herself. Just then she heard a sudden sharp noise, at the far end of the row of stalls. If she hadn't known that there were no horses now at Balnacraig (except for Lucky down at the farm), she could have sworn it was the sound of a hoof stamping upon the cobbled floor.

She looked at her parents. They were smiling.

"Your present is an especially big one," they said.

"For Christmas and for your eighth birthday."

"Have a look down at the far end."

Sophie plodded down the stable till she came to the end stall, the one with the name FRISK above it.

There stood Lucky.

"What's Lucky doing up here?" said Sophie. "Why isn't he down at the farm?"

"Because he doesn't live there anymore," her mother said.

"Because we bought him from the Grants," said her father.

Sophie gulped.

"For me?" she said.

"For you," they said. "For your very own."

For once Sophie didn't shout, "Yikes!"

For once she wasn't able to speak at all.

At last she managed to mutter in a rather strangled voice, "Thanks, Mommy. Thanks, Dad," and she patted them both. Then she went to pat Lucky.

"Hello again, my dear," she said, and she put an arm around his neck and gave him a hug, and looked up at her father and mother and grinned all over her face.

"Hello again, my dear," said Sophie.

"Happy?" they said.

"I'm the happiest," said Sophie, "that I've ever been in the whole of my life."

THE

END

F   King-Smith, Dick
KIN   Sophie's Lucky

copy 2

LOWELL SCHOOL

**Lowell School
1640 Kalmia Rd NW
Washington DC 20012**

NOV 20 1997